Z FOR ZARAY

Zaray Brown

I am **A**wesome.

Brilliant also describes me.

I am azzling in any room.

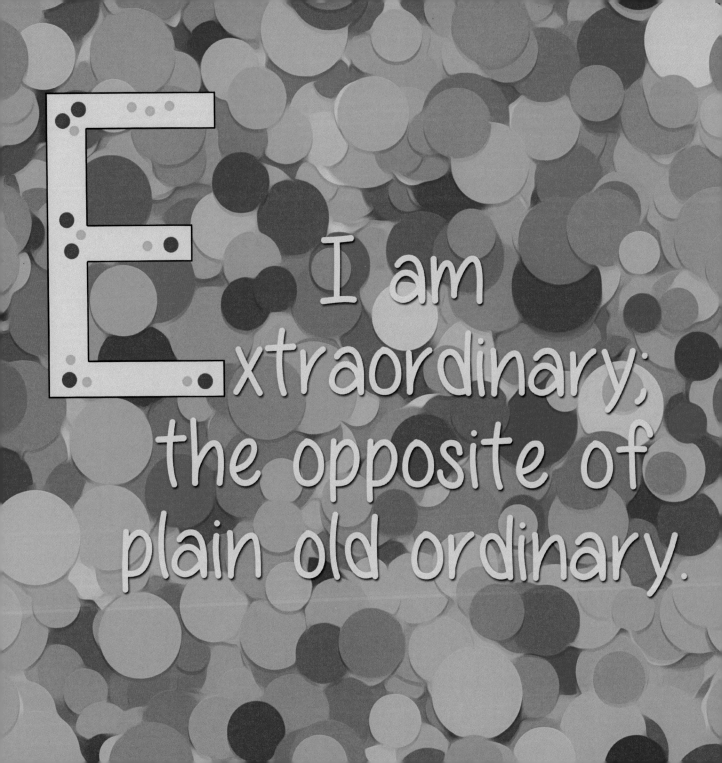

E I am Extraordinary, the opposite of plain old ordinary.

F

I am Fancy, just look at my shoes.

I am
Glad to be me

Happier than I can ever be.

I am Intelligent.

My life is filled with

Joy

I am Kind.

I love to Laugh.

I have a Magical life

I Am **N**ice

I am

Outstanding.

I am Patient with my little brother.

I **Q**uickly help others.

My smile is

R adiant.

I am especially

Special.

I have many Talents.

SWIMMER

ACROBATIC

DANCER

SINGER

ACTRESS

I am Unique.

I am Valuable.

I am Youthful

I am

Zaray